CAM JANSEN

and the
Mystery of the
Stolen Diamonds

★ ★

DAVID A. ADLER
Illustrated by Susanna Natti

★ ★

SCHOLASTIC INC.
New York Toronto London Auckland Sydney

ISBN 0-590-29315-X (meets NASTA specifications)

Text copyright © 1980 by David A. Adler. Illustrations copyright © 1980 by Susanna Natti. All rights reserved. Published by Scholastic Inc., 730 Broadway, New York, NY 10003, by arrangement with Viking Penguin, a division of Penguin Books USA Inc.

2 3 4 5 6 7 8 9 10   40   00 99 98 97 96 95 94

Printed in the U.S.A.

First Scholastic printing, September 1992

The *Cam Jansen Adventure* series

To Deborah Brodie, a good friend

Cam Jansen and the
Mystery of the Stolen Diamonds

Chapter One

It was the first morning of spring vacation. Cam Jansen and her friend Eric Shelton were sitting on a bench in the middle of a busy shopping mall. While Eric's mother was shopping, they were watching Eric's baby brother, Howie. And they were playing a memory game.

Eric's eyes were closed.

"What color jacket am I wearing?" Cam asked.

"Blue."

"Wrong. I'm not wearing a jacket."

Eric opened his eyes. "It's no use," he said. "I'll never have a memory like yours."

"You have to keep practicing," Cam told him. "Now try me."

Cam looked straight ahead. She said, *"Click,"* and then closed her eyes. Cam always said, *"Click,"* when she wanted to remember something. She said it was the sound her mental camera made when it took a picture.

Eric looked for something he could be sure Cam hadn't noticed. Then he asked, "What does the sign in the card store window say?"

"That's easy. 'Mother's Day Sunday May 11. Remember your mother and she'll remember you.'"

"You win," Eric said.

Cam still had her eyes closed. "Come on, ask me something else."

Cam had what people called a photographic memory. Her mind took a picture

of whatever she saw. Once, she forgot her notebook in school. She did her home-work—ten math problems—all from the picture of the assignment she had stored in her brain.

When Cam was younger, people called her Jennifer. That's her real name. But when they found out about her amazing memory, they started calling her "The Camera." Soon "The Camera" was shortened to "Cam."

"All right," Eric said. "What color socks am I wearing?"

Cam thought a moment. "That's not really fair," she said. "I never saw your socks."

But Cam didn't open her eyes. "You're wearing green pants, a green belt, and green sneakers," she said. "I'll bet your socks are green, too."

"You're too much, Cam."

"No, you're too neat."

"It's my turn now," Eric said.

Eric looked carefully at all the stores and people in the shopping mall. He closed his eyes. But he quickly opened them again. Howie was crying.

"What do we do now?" Cam asked. "Should I look for your mother?"

6

Eric shook his head. "Let's wait. Maybe Howie will go back to sleep."

"But what if he doesn't?" Cam asked.

"Then I have to find out whether he wants to be held, fed, or changed. I have everything I need right here." Eric patted the insulated bag strapped to the front of the carriage.

Eric and Cam watched to see what Howie would do. He squirmed, turned his head from side to side, and then went back to sleep.

"Let's play another memory game," Cam said.

"Let's not. I'm tired of losing." Eric rocked the carriage. "Rocking relaxes a baby," he told Cam.

Cam was an only child so she didn't know much about babies. Eric was the oldest of four children. Besides Howie, who wasn't even a year old, Eric had twin sisters who were seven.

Eric rocked the carriage gently while he and Cam talked about the fifth-grade science fair. It was being held right after spring vacation. Eric was making a sundial, and Cam was making a box camera.

Suddenly a loud bell rang. It woke Howie and he started to cry.

Cam jumped up on the bench. "It's Parker's Jewelry Store!" she yelled. "Their alarm just went off."

Eric pulled at Cam's sneakers. "Get down from there."

"No, wait. Maybe something is happening."

Something *was* happening. A tall, heavy man with a mustache and wearing a dark suit ran out of the jewelry store toward the center of the mall. He was in a real hurry. He pushed people aside—including Eric. Cam looked straight at the man and said, *"Click."*

Chapter Two

The man kept running and caused a great commotion. He was bumping into dozens of people. He left a path of angry shoppers from Parker's Jewelry Store halfway through the shopping mall.

"Come back here, young man," one woman shouted, "and pick up all my packages!"

Another woman dropped a bag filled with groceries. Eggs broke. Tomatoes and cucumbers were rolling in all directions.

"If he's trying to get away," Cam asked,

"why didn't he run out one of the exits?"

"What?" Eric wasn't really listening. Howie was still crying, and Eric was trying to calm him.

Just then a young couple came out of the jewelry store.

"Look," Cam said. "They were inside when the alarm went off."

A small crowd had gathered. Cam was still standing on the bench. From there she had a good view of the entrance to Parker's.

The couple walked toward the nearest exit. The man was wearing a dark suit. He was tall, and so was the woman with him. She was holding what looked like a baby, wrapped in a pink blanket.

"There, there, baby," the woman was saying. "Don't cry. It's all over now. Don't cry."

The man was holding a very large pink-and-blue baby rattle. He was urging the

11

woman to walk faster. Cam looked straight
at them as they walked past, and said,
"*Click.*"

Then Eric saw two old women coming
out of the store.

"Look," he said, pointing. "They were in
there, too, when the alarm went off."

The women were upset. One was clutch-
ing her heart. The other was leaning for-
ward and holding a cane with both hands.
She walked as if the cane were the only
thing keeping her up.

The women sat down on the bench
nearest Cam and Eric. "Oh, my," the
woman holding her heart said. "I never
thought I'd live through that."

The other woman just sighed.

Cam watched the entrance to Parker's a while longer. No one else left the store. Then she saw someone inside shut the door and hang a sign in the window. The sign said, "Sorry, We're Closed."

"I wonder what happened," Cam said as she got down from the bench.

Eric rocked Howie in his arms. "I don't know, but I wish they'd shut off that alarm. It's scaring Howie. I'll have to feed him if he doesn't stop crying."

Eric held Howie against his shoulder. Howie stopped crying, but just for a minute. A loud police car siren sounded. It startled Howie, and he began to cry again.

"Quick, Cam, get me his bottle. It's in the insulated bag."

Cam opened the bag and looked inside. "Boy, he sure needs a lot of stuff."

She gave the bottle to Eric. "Are you sure you know how to feed him?"

"It's easy. Watch."

14

Eric cradled Howie in one arm. With his free hand he fed him the bottle. Howie was quiet.

"It works," Cam said. "I guess he can't cry and drink at the same time."

The siren got louder and louder.

"They must have called the police," Cam said. She watched as the police car turned into the mall parking lot and slowed down. It stopped in front of Parker's Jewelry Store.

Both front doors of the car opened. Two policemen got out and went inside Parker's. A moment later the alarm over the store stopped ringing.

"They better hurry," Cam said, "or they won't catch the man who ran out."

The police did hurry. In a very short time they came out of Parker's. They went over to the people standing just outside the store.

"Please, we need your cooperation," one

of the policemen said. "Did any of you see a man run from here?"

Everyone started yelling at once.

"Yes, we saw him."

"He was tall."

"Heavy."

"No. No. He was short. Short and thin."

"He had a mustache."

"He was wearing an ugly green tie."

"Ugly! I liked that tie. I have the same one at home."

The policeman held up his hands for quiet. "Did any of you see which way he went?"

"I did," one woman called out. "He almost knocked me down." She put her hands on her hips and waited to make sure everyone was listening. "He went that way." She pointed toward the center of the mall.

One policeman ran to the center of the mall. The other reached into the car. He pulled out a police phone and spoke into it.

"Robbery reported at Parker's Jewelry Store, Hamilton Shopping Mall. Suspect, wearing dark suit and green tie, was last seen running toward Stage Street exit. Please send car to Stage and Fulton to help apprehend. Ten-four, central."

He reached into the car and replaced the phone. Then he ran toward the center of the mall.

Chapter Three

Cam sat down on the bench. She ran her fingers through her hair. Cam had what people called bright red hair even though it was more orange than red. Eric's hair was dark brown.

"Do you think they'll catch him?" Eric asked.

"It shouldn't be too hard," Cam said. "Almost everyone between here and the other end of the mall saw which way he went."

Eric was still feeding Howie. "Are you almost finished?" Cam asked.

"Almost."

"Good. Then we can go ask those two old women what happened inside the jewelry store."

Eric took the bottle out of Howie's mouth and set it down on the bench. He held Howie against his shoulder and patted his back. Howie burped.

"Okay," Eric announced. "We're ready."

Eric carried Howie, and Cam pushed the carriage. They went over to the next bench.

"My, what a cute baby," the woman with the cane said. "Is it a boy or a girl?"

"Boy."

The woman looked straight at Howie and asked, "Where's your mother, little boy?"

"He doesn't talk yet," Eric told her.

"Oh."

"I'm his brother. My mother took the twins shopping for clothes. I'm watching him until they're done."

"Clothes. Well, they're lucky they're not shopping for jewelry."

"Why?" Cam asked. "What happened inside the jewelry store?"

The woman put her hand to her cheek. She shook her head slowly. "Oh, it was horrible. We were there when a man came in and pointed a gun right at Mr. Parker. 'Diamonds,' he said. 'Every loose one you got.'

"Mr. Parker gave him a whole pile of small diamonds. You know, the kind he uses to make earrings. The man took them all. Then he made Mr. Parker lie face down on the floor.

"Isn't that right, Esther?"

"Yes," the other woman said, nodding her head. "He was terribly impolite."

"Then," the first woman went on, "he pointed his gun straight at us. He didn't dare talk to us the way he talked to Mr. Parker. He didn't rob us either. He just said, 'Ladies, turn around and face the wall and you won't get hurt.'

"There was a nice young couple in the store too. They had their baby with them, a cute little girl. I heard the man with the gun tell them to face the wall, too.

"It was horrible. We stayed that way,

with our faces to the wall, until Mr. Parker told us it was safe to leave."

The woman stopped talking. Someone was shouting. They all turned to see where the noise was coming from.

The policemen were coming back. There were four of them now. Handcuffed to one policeman was a tall man in a dark suit.

"I didn't do it!" the man yelled. "You've got the wrong man!"

"We'll let Mr. Parker decide that," the policeman said.

Cam was all excited. "That's him! They got him! That's the man who ran out of Parker's. I remember that mustache, that dark suit, and that ugly green tie."

"Well, he may be the man who ran out of the store," the woman with the cane declared, "but he's not the man who robbed Mr. Parker. Is he, Esther?"

"No. That's not him. I'm sure of it."

Chapter Four

Cam and Eric went back to their bench and sat down. Eric put Howie in the carriage and rocked him to sleep.

"Do you think those women are right?" Eric asked. "Do you think the police caught the wrong man?"

"The whole thing doesn't make sense," Cam said. "Whoever robbed the store pointed his gun straight at those women. They should know what he looks like. But if they're right and the man isn't the thief, why did he run like that?"

"Maybe you were wrong. Maybe he's not the man we saw running."

"Oh, he's the man all right," Cam said. "The man who ran past us had a mustache that curled up at the ends and an ugly green tie with red and yellow flowers. I'm sure that's the man the police caught."

The small crowd was gone. The only evidence that something had happened was the police car and the "Sorry, We're

Closed" sign in the window of the jewelry store. The four policemen and the man they caught were all inside Parker's.

Cam got up on the bench. She closed her eyes.

"What are you doing up there?" Eric asked.

"Thinking. This is where I was when everything happened. Standing here should help me remember what I saw."

"You know," Eric said, "there was another man who left the store, the man with the baby."

Cam sat down. "Yes, I know. I have a picture of him in my brain. He was tall and wore a dark suit just like the man the police caught. And he was holding a large baby rattle."

Cam thought for a minute. Then she went to the front of Howie's carriage and opened the insulated bag.

Cam spoke slowly, as if she were talking

and thinking at the same time. "There was something strange about that couple. Your mother packs this whole bag when she takes Howie somewhere. That couple had a baby too, but all they brought along was a rattle."

Cam stopped talking. Something was happening inside the store. Mr. Parker came to the window and turned the "closed" sign around. The other side of the sign said, "We're Open. Come in and Browse."

The door opened. The policemen came out with the man they had caught. He was no longer handcuffed. They spoke to him for just a moment. Then the man walked away. He walked past Cam and Eric and out the nearest exit. He smiled as he walked by.

"They let him go!" Cam said.

"Yeah, but did you see which way he went!"

Cam looked at Eric. They were both thinking the same thing.

"Before, when he was in such a rush, he went that way." Eric pointed to the center of the mall. "If he was in such a hurry to get there before, you'd think he'd go back that way now."

"Yeah," Cam said, "but he's going in the other direction. And it's the same way that couple went. Something strange is going on. Come on, let's follow him!"

"But what about Howie?"

"Bring him along."

Chapter Five

Cam and Eric quickly went out the Lee Avenue exit, the same one the man had gone through a few minutes earlier. It led to a street crowded with shoppers leaving the mall.

"Do you see him?" Eric asked.

"I think so. I think that's him up ahead. He's starting to walk down Lee Avenue."

Cam and Eric tried to get through the crowd quickly. With a baby carriage it wasn't easy.

They brushed past a woman carrying a

few large packages. She lost her balance,
and one of the packages fell.

"What do you think that is," she yelled,
pointing to the carriage, "a hot rod?"

Eric picked up the package. "I'm sorry,"
he told the woman.

"You should be, running through here
like that. I hope you don't have a baby in
there."

Eric was about to tell her there was a baby in the carriage. Cam didn't let him.

"Come on," she urged, "or we'll lose the man."

They rushed ahead. They turned the corner onto Lee Avenue and saw the man halfway down the block.

"Let's not get too close," Eric warned Cam, "or he'll know we're following him."

They were careful to keep a good distance behind the man. It didn't help. When the man reached the corner, he turned and looked straight at them.

"He saw us," Eric whispered. "What should we do?"

"Keep walking. If we stop whenever he does, he'll know we're following him."

The man stood still and waited. After Cam and Eric pushed the baby carriage past him, he turned and walked down Minnow Road.

Cam and Eric kept walking until the man

was out of sight. Then they turned and walked back to the corner of Minnow Road. The street was filled with construction equipment and huge mounds of dirt. A row of old houses was being torn down. Cam and Eric saw the man walk into the last house at the far end of the street.

"It's almost twelve," Eric said. "My mother will be waiting. Let's go back and call the police."

"And what would we tell them? If those women and Mr. Parker are right, we're following an innocent man. As soon as we know something we'll call."

Cam crouched and made her way down the street. "Come on," she called in a loud whisper.

Eric crouched, too, as he pushed Howie's carriage and followed Cam.

There were piles of dirt and sand all along the sidewalk. When they were behind a huge mound of dirt in front of the

last house, Cam collapsed. "We made it," she said.

"What do we do now?"

"Let's see what's going on inside that house."

Cam and Eric started to crawl up the dirt pile. Then Eric stopped. Howie was no longer sleeping. He was beginning to move in his carriage.

"Keep him quiet," Cam whispered.

"I'll try."

"You better do more than try. If he cries we're in real trouble."

Eric rocked the carriage gently. Howie looked up at Eric, but he didn't cry.

Cam reached the top of the dirt pile. She had a good view of the old house. It was three stories high with rows of windows. Some of the windows were broken. There were no curtains or shades. Cam could see right inside.

Through a large window on the first

floor she saw the man they had followed.
He wasn't alone. The couple who had left
the jewelry store just after the robbery was
there, too.

Cam quickly crawled down the hill. "I
was right, Eric."

"Sh." Eric pointed to Howie. "I think
he's going back to sleep."

"They're all in there," Cam whispered, "the Runner and the couple we saw leaving the store. They're all working together. The Runner made all that commotion to keep the police from catching the real thief."

"What about the woman and the baby?"

"Maybe they figured no one would suspect a man who went shopping with his wife and baby. If they did, they were right. You saw what happened when they left the store. They just walked away, and almost no one noticed."

"Let's go back now," Eric urged, "and get the police."

"You go," Cam told him, "and hurry! I'll stay here and watch the house."

"Watch Howie, too. I can move faster without him."

Eric ran off before Cam could tell him she didn't know how to watch a baby.

Cam sat back against the pile of dirt and

waited. It was very quiet. Cam looked around. Then she saw why it was so quiet. There were barriers at both ends of the street. Because houses were being torn down, cars were not allowed on Minnow Road.

Cam realized that she and Howie were alone. The only other people nearby were the thieves. *I hope Eric hurries,* Cam thought.

Whoosh!

Something dropped to the ground. Cam looked up. A squirrel running along the branch of a tree had dropped an acorn.

Howie started to cry. *Oh, no!* Cam thought. *What would Eric do?*

Cam said, *"Click."* Sometimes just saying it helped her remember. It did. Cam remembered the insulated bag and that Howie couldn't drink milk and cry at the same time. She took the bottle out of the bag.

Then Cam heard another noise. She dropped the bottle and looked up. This time it wasn't a squirrel.

Chapter Six

A big tall man was standing on top of the mound of dirt. He was wearing an ugly green tie and had a mustache that curled up at the ends. It was the Runner.

"Well," he growled, "look who we have here—the baby sitter and her baby. Where's your friend?"

"He . . . he went home."

"If you were smart you would've done the same thing. Let's go."

Cam carried Howie up the front steps of the house. Inside, the house was musty.

The floor was covered with dust and littered with old newspapers and magazines. The Runner took Cam and Howie into a large room.

"Look what I got," the Runner said. "It's one of the kids I saw following me."

A man and a woman looked up. It was the couple Cam had seen leaving Parker's Jewelry Store. They were sitting in worn, old-fashioned easy chairs. There was a small table between them.

"You said there were two of them," the sitting man snapped. "Where's the other one?"

"He wasn't out there," the Runner said.

"Great! Everything was perfect until you get yourself followed. Well, watch this kid. Don't let her get away."

The Runner nudged Cam and Howie into a corner. He stood there watching them. Cam looked at the thieves and was frightened.

"Let's divide this stuff and get out of here," the sitting man said.

He took a large baby rattle out of his pocket. It was the rattle he was carrying as he left the store. He screwed off the top and carefully emptied the contents onto the table.

"Wow!" the woman said.

That was exactly how Cam felt. The rattle was filled with diamonds. They sparkled as the man started to count them.

"One, two, three . . ."

Cam held Howie close and looked around the room. In the back, pulled away from the wall, were a few large bookcases. There were windows behind the bookcases. And there was an open door, which led to another room.

Cam looked at the thieves. Something was missing. She whispered, *"Click,"* and tried to remember what it was.

The baby, she thought. *Where's the baby?*

Then Cam noticed something on the floor wrapped in a pink blanket. It was a large doll. Cam realized that there never was a baby. That's why the couple hadn't been carrying any of the things Eric's mother packed in the insulated bag. The thieves had taken the doll along so they would look like a family. And the rattle was a good place to hide the diamonds.

The man was still counting. "Fifty-eight, fifty-nine, sixty . . ."

Cam looked at her watch. It was 12:30. *Where's Eric?* she thought. *Maybe he can't get the police to come.*

"Seventy-nine, eighty, eighty-one. We got eighty-one diamonds," the man announced.

"Let's see now," he said as he did some figuring on an old newspaper. "That's eighty-one divided by three. Hmm. That gives each of us twenty-one. No, that's not right." He did some more figuring.

"Twenty-seven," the woman said. "We each get twenty-seven."

The Runner left Cam's side and went to get his diamonds.

I can't wait for Eric, Cam thought. *This is my chance.*

She held Howie tight and ran to the door in the back of the room. She slammed the door shut as if she were leaving the room. Then she jumped behind the nearest bookcase.

"Get her!" someone yelled.

Cam hoped her trick would work. She couldn't see what was happening, but she heard doors opening and closing and a lot of yelling.

"Find her!"

"I'm looking."

"Check the back room."

The trick did work. The thieves thought she had left the room. They were looking all over the house for her.

Cam knew she couldn't stay behind that bookcase forever. Eventually the thieves would find her. She looked at Howie. His eyes were open. *Or you might cry,* Cam thought.

There was a window behind the bookcase. Cam tried to open it. She couldn't. It was jammed.

The window behind the next bookcase was open, but to get to it Cam would have to run past a large open area. Cam didn't know if anyone else was in the room. She was afraid to run out in the open.

Someone ran past the bookcase.

"What about the kitchen?"

"I've already looked there."

"Look again."

Howie began to stir. *Oh, no!* Cam thought. *He's getting ready to cry!*

Chapter Seven

The bottle! Cam thought. *I should have taken it along. That would keep him quiet.*

Then Cam had an idea. She gently pushed the tip of her finger into Howie's mouth. The baby was quiet as he sucked on Cam's finger.

Cam heard footsteps. One of the men was standing very close.

"You check the cellar," the man yelled. "I'll look in here."

Cam heard the man move slowly around

the room. Then it was quiet. Cam wondered where the man had gone.

"Psst . . . Psst."

The sound came from behind. Cam was afraid to look.

"Psst . . . Psst. Over here. Hurry."

It didn't sound like one of the thieves. Cam turned. Through the open window behind the next bookcase she saw the head and shoulders of a policeman. He was sig-

naling for Cam to run over and climb out.

Cam held Howie tightly. She ran past the open area, then squeezed into the small space between the window and the bookcase. She handed Howie to the policeman. Then she climbed out and jumped to the ground.

Eric ran up and took Howie in his arms. Howie looked at the policeman, then at Eric, then back at the policeman. Then Howie started to cry.

Cam smiled. "Boy, am I glad he didn't do that inside!"

"Yes, I'm sure you are," the policeman said.

Another policeman ran up to them. He was carrying a megaphone.

"How many of them are in there?"

"Three. Two men and a woman."

"That's what your friend told us."

Cam and Eric went behind one of the police cars. "I'm sure glad you're all right,"

Eric said. "I got back here as fast as I could."

The policeman held the megaphone to his mouth. "This is the police. The house is surrounded. Come out with your hands up."

Cam looked around. The house *was* surrounded. She saw about fifteen policemen and four other police cars parked around the house.

"Come out with your hands up and you won't get hurt."

The back door opened. First the woman came out and then the two men. They all had their hands up. The policemen handcuffed them and led them into one of the police cars.

Chapter Eight

One of the policemen drove Cam, Eric, and Howie back to the shopping mall. Howie's carriage was tied to the roof of the car.

"You must be 'The Camera,' " the policeman said to Cam. "Your friend told us about your amazing memory.

"Well, it's lucky you were in the mall," the policeman went on. "Those thieves had us baffled. Mr. Parker told us there was only one thief. So, of course, we chased the one man who ran. Mr. Parker was lying on the floor. Those two old ladies were facing the wall. None of them saw the thief join up with a woman and pretend to be part of a young family out shopping."

The policeman drove the car through the shopping mall parking lot. He parked it right in front of Parker's Jewelry Store. Eric's mother and sisters were waiting for them. So were the two old women.

As soon as the police car stopped, Eric's mother ran over and opened the door. She quickly took Howie in her arms.

"Eric and Jennifer, it's one o'clock. Where have you been?"

"Your mother has been worried sick," the old woman with the cane said.

"These two are heroes," the policeman said, pointing to Cam and Eric. "They helped us capture the gang that robbed the jewelry store."

"You know," the woman with the cane said, "there was a nice young couple in Par-

ker's when the store was robbed. I remember that cute baby they had. Well, someone should tell them the robbers have been caught. They may be worried."

"Nice couple!" Cam yelled. Then she laughed. Eric and the policeman laughed, too.